S0-AHU-054

THE
CLASS TRIP
FROM THE
BLACK LAGOON

THE
CLASS TRIP
FROM THE
BLACK LAGOON

by Mike Thaler
Illustrated by Jared Lee

SCHOLASTIC INC.

New York   Toronto   London   Auckland   Sydney
Mexico City   New Delhi   Hong Kong   Buenos Aires

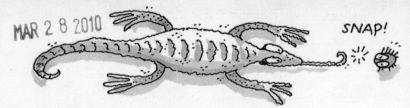

SNAP!

For Ruwan Jayatilleke,
a dedication to your dedication.
—M.T.

For Stephanie, Cassy, Zachery, Danielle, and
Garrett
—J.L.

ISBN-13: 978-0-439-42927-6
ISBN-10: 0-439-42927-7

27 26 25 24 23 22 21 20 19   8 9 10 11 12 13/0
Printed in the U.S.A.
First printing, September 2002

CONTENTS

CHAPTER 1
THE NEWS BLUES

We're going to take a class trip tomorrow. It's our first class trip. I hope it's a *first-class* trip!

I've read about the Titanic. Only the first-class passengers got the good food and lifeboats. I hope we don't hit a giant ice cube and go down the sink.

Maybe we won't take a boat at all. Maybe we'll fly on an airplane. I still don't know what holds those things up. Then again, maybe we'll take a train. I know what holds them up . . . bandits!

They say, "Getting there is half the fun." What's the other half? Getting back, of course!

CHAPTER 2
EXPLORING THE SUBJECT

In my history book, I learned a lot about some famous class trips. Lewis and Clark's class went across America. They couldn't find one open motel.

A kid named Chris Columbus
sailed across the ocean. He got
very seasick.

Marco Polo walked to China.
He met a real emperor.

Richard Byrd's class went to the South Pole. They met a real emperor penguin.

QUACK!

WE COME IN PEACE.

And Neil Armstrong went all the way to the moon. He didn't meet anybody.

I wonder where we're going and whom we're going to meet.

CHAPTER 3
DESTINATION SPECULATION

Freddy calls. We talk about all the possibilities. Then we pick our favorite one. Freddy wants to go to *Pizza Mutt*. I choose *Dizzyland*.

16

But we'll probably be going to
the nature museum or the art
museum. At one, you look at the
charts, and at the other, you look
at the arts.

Freddy still holds out for Pizza Mutt. He always looks on the bright side. He's an *optometrist*.

18

Then Eric calls. He always looks on the dark side. He's what they call a *messymist*.

He says that there's a 50-percent accident rate on class trips.

Half the class will be carried off by wild animals, fall off a high mountain, or drop into a deep hole. We choose our favorite. We both pick dropping into a deep hole, so we can pretend to be golf balls.

Then Randy calls and says that sometimes you go to *really* dangerous places. Your parents have to sign a release form.

One class went on a picnic to an active volcano. It erupted and all they ever found were 15 toasted peanut butter and jelly sandwiches.

Another class took a trip to Antarctica. Is there an *uncle-arctica* and *cousin-arcticas*? They're still defrosting.

My mom says that the first place I have to go is to bed because I have to get up early tomorrow morning.

CHAPTER 4
WONDER ENLIGHTENING

It's hard to fall asleep. I keep thinking about all the places we could go. And I worry about all the things that could happen.

We might make a journey to the center of the earth. But in the middle, it's like the hot fudge on a sundae.

I don't even like to go into a closet. I'm happier when I can see the sky. Eric says I have *closet-ra-phobia*. If we go far enough, then we'll come out in China. Then we could eat lunch at a Chinese restaurant.

Or maybe we'll just go to the bottom of the ocean. There are many things down there with lots of teeth and lots of arms. It's also very dark. The deepest that I've ever been in the ocean is up to my ankles.

Maybe we'll go to Mars. They put you to sleep, and when you wake up . . . you're there.

The things on Mars are even weirder than the things at the bottom of the ocean.

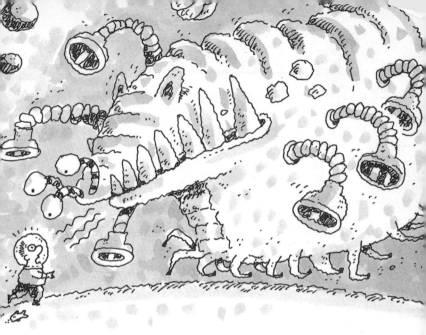

They've got bigger teeth, longer arms like springs, and fingers like plungers. Their eyeballs are on stalks and wave around in the air. They all have bad breath and breathe through their ears. You have to put your head in a fishbowl and walk around in slow motion.

27

Where in the world are we going to go? Or where out of the world? I close my eyes and wonder. . . .

CHAPTER 5
THIS MUST BE D-DAY

The alarm goes off at 5:30 *in the morning*! I hate getting up early. The chickens aren't even up yet! And I shuffle into the bathroom.

My eyes are hardly open. I squeeze out some toothpaste and brush my teeth. Boy, it sure tastes weird. I look at the tube and it says BROWN SHOE POLISH.

My shirt feels very small. Then I discover that my head is in the sleeve. My pants feel odd, too. I discover they are on backward. At least I won't mess up with my shoes. Wrong again! I have the left one on my right foot. And the right one's on my knee. This is not going to be a great day.

31

CHAPTER 6
OFF WE GO

I wonder what I should pack. Randy says that you have to be prepared for anything. He says that he's taking snowshoes, malaria pills, signal flares, a snakebite kit, and a lifeboat.

I think I'll take my lucky rabbit's foot. Of course, it wasn't lucky for the rabbit.

Oh, well. I stumble downstairs for breakfast. I grab a box of cereal and pour some into a bowl. Then I pour in some milk. It all bubbles up. I look at the cereal box. It says DISHWASHING POWDER. . . . I guess I'll skip breakfast.

I open the front door and step outside. It's dark and full of coats. Wrong door. I try again and really step outside. It is just as dark but there are no coats. Even the early birds aren't up yet. I feel like an early worm and wiggle to the corner.

I wait there with my brown teeth chattering. Out of the gloom come two lights. It's the school bus. Mr. Fenderbender opens the door and I get on.

All the kids are there, sitting stiff and staring straight ahead. They all have brown teeth. Everybody's breath smells horrible. A green fog covers all the windows. I guess we won't be singing camp songs today.

MOVE IT!

SCHOOL BUS

BANG!

After four minor collisions, Mr. Fenderbender stops and tells us to get out. Things have to get better . . . don't they?

CHAPTER 7
INTO THE WILD BLUE YONDER

We're at a small airfield. Mrs. Green is standing by the first passenger plane ever made. It says BUILT BY THE WRONG BROTHERS on the side.

As we climb aboard, she hands each of us a parachute. I guess we're not going to the museum. We strap them on and try to sit in our seats. I feel like a camel.

Mr. Fenderbender puts on a pilot's cap with goggles and sits up front with Mrs. Green. They both try to figure out how to start the plane.

Meanwhile, Eric, the class clown, pretends to be the flight attendant and gives the safety instructions. "In case of the *likely* event of a water landing, your seat cushion can be used as a flotation unit." I look down. There is no seat cushion. This is definitely not first class.

Doris asks what movie will be playing. "We're showing a bunch of selected shorts," Eric answers. He smiles and then reaches into his backpack and pulls out his underwear. "Gross!" we yell.

41

Mr. Fenderbender guns the engine. We're all pressed back in our seats. "Happy landings," cackles Mrs. Green.

CHAPTER 8
FLYING HIGH

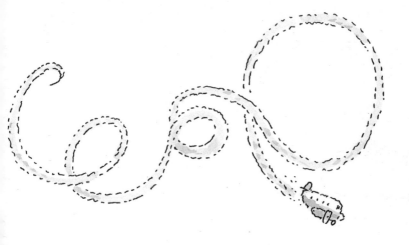

Mr. Fenderbender flies like he drives. We do loop-de-loops, barrel rolls, and dives. Penny throws up. Good thing I didn't eat breakfast.

PUKE BAG

After eight hours of aerial acrobatics, a red light goes on. Mrs. Green lines us up alphabetically, opens the door, checks our parachutes, and then pushes us out. Derek is first, but I'm secooooooond!

We land all over—east, west, north, and south. There are kids twisted in every possible gymnastic position. Mrs. Green grades us on our landings. Freddy is the only one who gets an F. He landed in a lion's mouth.

We are all a little shorter as we line up and march off into the jungle. The lion burps. Freddy would have liked that.

CHAPTER 9
JUNGLE BUNGLE

The jungle is having a bad hair day. It takes every blade in my Swiss Army knife to hack our way through.

And you have to be *very* careful where you step. All the animals are party poopers, and you have to look out for the dreaded *hippo-potty-mess*.

The heat beats down on us. It's like being in a furry oven.

All of a sudden, Eric shouts out, "Knock, knock!"

"Who's there?" we all ask.

Eric beats his chest and yells, "Tarzan!"

"Tarzan who?" we ask.

"Tarzan stripes forever!" he giggles.

I guess that's a little jungle joke.

49

A snake as long as a jumbo jet slides by. Hairy spiders as big as hamsters bounce on webs as large as trampolines.

Penny sniffs a purple flower and it grabs the end of her nose. Mrs. Green tells us the name of the plant in Latin. She says we'll have a quiz in an hour.

Randy sees a sandbox and jumps in. Unfortunately, it's a quicksand box. He sinks in up to his chin. "It's not recess yet," scolds Mrs. Green as she pulls him out.

Derek pets an orange zebra with black stripes. Mrs. Green tells him it's a tiger and that he doesn't have to raise his hand anymore if he has a question.

Mosquitoes as big as Count Dracula buzz all around us. They think it's lunchtime and that we're the special of the day. I feel like we're in an all-you-can-eat restaurant, and we're on the menu!

Eric shouts, "Knock, knock!"
"Who's there?" we all ask.
"Safari," he says.
We throw up our hands.
"Safari who?" we ask.
"Why do we have to walk safari?!" he laughs.

CHAPTER 10
FAST FOOD

Finally, we reach a river and cross it by stepping on crocodiles. One eats Doris's backpack and all. I guess that's the toll. It's sort of a potluck dinner. Without any luck . . . we'll be the dinner. I hope that a giraffe doesn't swallow me. The fall could be huge—or worse, I could be sucked up an elephant's nose. *Snot* a nice way to go!

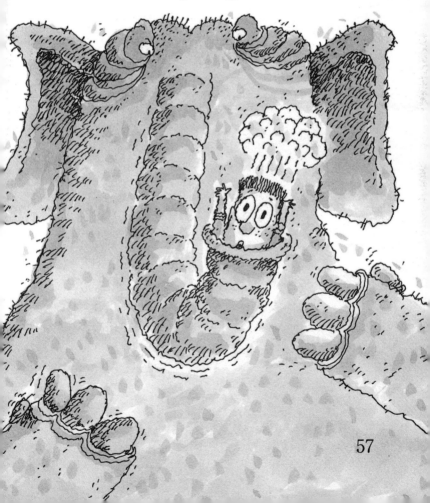

I don't want to be a baboon's breakfast, a lion's lunch, a crocodile's dinner, or a snake's snack. I run and hold up a sign that says PLEASE DON'T FEED THE ANIMALS. I hope they can read.

CHAPTER 11
IN THE GRAND SAND

By noon, we come to a desert. The good news is there's no more jungle. The bad news is there's a lot of sand. We're very thirsty. Unfortunately, there are no public water fountains. The only good thing about a desert is that if you add another *s* it would be a *dessert*!

Kids are dropping like flies. I've never seen a fly drop, but I've seen fly droppings. Anyway, it's hot, and it's lunchtime.

I even miss the school cafeteria. I'm losing it. I ask if we can stop and eat. "Not until the lunch bell rings," says Mrs. Green. I hear a lot of bells.

Then I start seeing things. . . . A Pizza Mutt wiggling in the heat waves. A swimming pool full of rubber ducks.

I even see a school bus. Wait, it *is* a school bus! It drives up. On the front of it are printed the words **CLASS TRIP**.

Mr. Fenderbender opens the door and I get on. All the kids are sitting there bright-eyed and excited.

Mrs. Green says we're going to the zoo to see a lot of wild animals. Hey, that's baby stuff. They're all in cages. A zoo is pretty tame after you've seen the real thing.

Maybe next time we'll blast off to a space station, climb Mount Everest, or water-ski up the Amazon River.

Now *that* would be a *trip*!